Days of Faithfulness

*When God proves His love
For His children*

Annette Gaddy Harper

Cranberry Quill Publishing, Inc.
P.O. Box 26227
Fayetteville, North Carolina 28314

Publisher's Note: Unless otherwise noted, all scripture references are taken from the King James and New King James Versions.

Layout and design by D. Renee Gibbs
Cover design by Jeff Davidson
Interior photography by Vaughn Jennings/ Scriptures on Pictures
Editors: Suzetta Perkins and Tammy Moody

Days of Faithfulness:
When God proves His love for His children. -- 1st ed.
ISBN: 978-0-578-41046-3

SPECIAL THANKS

To my Lord and Savior, for helping me to accomplish the dream.

To my Father, Ernest Pittman Gaddy – Thank you for your love and support.

To my husband, Steve – Thank you for your unconditional love, thoughtfulness and support.

To my family and friends – Thank you for your love and prayers.

To my editor, Suzetta Perkins – Thank you for your encouragement and inspiration to share this story.

To my editor, Tammy Moody – Thank you for your help and encouragement.

To Dr. Robert Appel Fayetteville Urology, Associates – Thank you for providing information to assist me with this story.

To Dr. Peter L. Villani, Lumberton Surgical Associates; Dr. Mahmood, Oncologist, Gibson Cancer Center, Lumberton, North Carolina; Dr. Sini Naik, Pulmonary Specialist, Lumberton, North Carolina; Duke Medical Center Cardiologists, Durham, North Carolina.

DEDICATION

This book is dedicated to my great-nephew, Tristan Ernest Thompson, who was named in honor of my father, Ernest. Tristan was born three months early on April 19, 2017 and thanks to God, the generous love and support from the staff at St. Mary's Hospital in Richmond, Virginia and from family and friends, Tristan continues to strive to live strong. This is a reminder to all that in the midst of trouble and pain, our faith in God will give us strength and eternal hope to overcome the difficult times in our life. So trust God to guide you because He understands the struggles we face.

May this story encourage you to remain faithful and to pray. Healing is in the name of Jesus. Through our suffering our faith is strengthened.

"Fear not, for I am with you; Be not dismayed, for I am your God. I will strengthen you, Yes, I will help you, I will uphold you with My righteous right hand."
Isaiah 41:10

—AGH

~ REVIEWS ~

Annette G. Harper has a unique ability to blend an intriguing story of faith, love, and family. The journey she shares with her father is a captivating story. She shares enough details to make her experiences feel intimately personal, without being clunky with the oversaturation of information. Readers are allowed to step inside the mind and heart of someone dealing with faith in times of crisis. You also have light-hearted moments, like the "disappearing bullet" moment of the story. Annette's faith in God and love of her family, create a rhythmic flow that carries the reader throughout the narrative. The miraculous highs and deep-felt lows resonate with you long after you finish reading it. People are busier than ever. Fortunately, reading this story took minimal time, but can have a massive positive impact on your life.

**~ Christoppher D. Stackhouse, Sr., Pastor
Lewis Chapel Missionary Baptist Church**

This is a very well-written book about two cancers a father had to overcome. I felt like I was there on this journey with the author. Mrs. Harper is so vivid and detailed in her writing. I believe that anyone reading this book will become a part of the story.

The one thing that I differ with the author is that God put these conditions on her father to test him. III John 1:2 states, "Beloved, I wish above all things that thou mayest prosper and be in health, even as thy soul prospereth." In chapter 9, Mrs. Harper confirms this very fact.

This is a true story; a very good book. Well written. Now, I look for the happily ever after book.

~ Sussie Sutton, Public Health Educator
B.S. Community Health Education
M.S.A Health Services Administration

<u>Days of Faithfulness</u> *is a story of hope and faith that will inspire and encourage those who may go through a difficult, tumultuous, or heartbreaking time in their lives. The Gaddy family's strength and endurance during the medical trials of their loved one, especially when hope and faith sometimes seemed elusive, is a testament to family resilience, a strong belief in God and love that never fails. This story gripped me to my core and I couldn't stop thinking about the power of God and how He manifests Himself through us to show who He is and can be in our lives.*
~ Author Suzetta Perkins

Faithfulness is the concept of remaining loyal to someone or something and putting loyalty into constant practice, regardless of the extenuating circumstances. It is the state of being full of faith and a sense of devotion to a person. This short story is a profile in courage and in an absolute inspiration to all who will read it. Annette, there are so many people who need to hear and learn from your story. This short story is simple, yet powerfully effective. I can't wait to share this story with family, friends and associates whom I know will absorb the lessons and use them in their everyday lives. Thanks for sharing your story of love and faithfulness. ~
~ Retired Colonel Donald Porter

PROLOGUE

In the autumn of the year 2005, my parents celebrated their 50th wedding anniversary with family and friends. My father, Ernest, was well aware of the anniversary celebration, but it was a surprise to my mother. Some secrets need to be kept. My father kept this secret for almost a year. It was a wonderful occasion to share with family and friends. *Jet* magazine featured a picture of my parents titled, "Golden Years" and President George Bush Jr.'s staff sent a letter to commemorate the day.

There's a turning point in everyone's life. The winter months were settling in and Father was scheduled for his yearly physical. In the past four years, he had neglected to schedule his prostate antigen (PSA) examination. He thought the doctor's office would inform him about his next visit. Somehow the paper trail was lost and it slipped Father's mind until he realized his colonoscopy examination was also due. In December of 2005, Father scheduled his colonoscopy examination with Dr. Augustine.

CONTENTS

THE NEWS

Early in the morning of December 14, 2005, my father called and said he would like to tell me something. I heard sadness in his voice, but I kept saying everything was all right. He told me his colonoscopy results were positive for colon cancer. I started thinking about a co-worker, who several years ago died of the same cancer. The kind of treatment Father was going to have or the scheduled surgery ahead hadn't crossed my mind. My only thought was being blessed for forty-seven years with Father and that his life expectancy would be shortened.

When the word cancer is introduced into our lives, the death phenomenon appears and our Christian faith disappears. My friend was a single mother with three young children, and I often wondered why God would take a mother away from her children since they're a blessing from God. However, we shouldn't question what God does but believe that everything will work out. God created us and our life is in His hands.

I was sitting around the table pondering what I should do about the news I'd received— cry, get mad with God, or accept the news and move on with life. Things happen for a reason...in season and out, and this was the season for me. My faith was tested, and in my mind, I believed God would bring me out of this darkness.

It was still December—chilly but not cold. The Christmas holidays were so wonderful with everyone sharing their joy of love. This is the time to be thankful for God's greatest gift— the birth of Jesus Christ. In spite of the holidays, work was busy, church was busy, and my family life was full of confusion. I didn't want to be bothered with news that would affect my lifestyle. But God makes things happen for all of us to wake up and realize it is not about me.

Father was advised by Dr. Augustine to talk with a surgeon. Dr. Augustine told Father that the cancer originated in the cecum and resembled the size of a bird's egg. The cecum is the blind pouch at the beginning of the large intestine into which the small intestine opens. He recommended Dr. Peter Villani as the best surgeon at Southeastern Medical Center in Lumberton, North Carolina.

Dr. Augustine's office made an appointment for Father for the second week of January, 2006. My mother, siblings, and I accompanied Father on his first visit. Dr. Villani explained the procedure in detail, and the operation was scheduled for January 16, 2006. Father had to be pre-certified to make sure everything was all right. He went to the anesthesiologist, who examined all of his records from Duke Medical Center. While observing his records, she found a small spot behind the heart and asked Father about it. He said that the cardiologist hadn't discussed the spot behind his heart.

Early Monday morning on January 16, 2006, Father's surgery was scheduled. My mother, brother, sister and I went to the hospital with Father. Uncle Nedward came by the hospital to see how Father was doing, but he was already in the pre-op room. Cousin Lane also came by. My husband called to see if everything was all right. I told him Father was in the pre-op room.

Dr. Villani entered the family waiting room and said everything was ready to go for the procedure. Father was prepped, capped, gowned, and given intravenous fluid (I.V.), as well as other medications. While in the operating room, Father said the anesthesiologist came in and said she was afraid to put him to sleep due to the spot behind his heart.

About one hour later, Dr. Villani came to the waiting room and informed the family that the surgery was cancelled. We looked surprised and puzzled at the news we'd received. I called my husband and told him the surgery was cancelled. My husband wanted to know why. I shared with him that Dr. Villani had told my father that he'd have to schedule an appointment with his cardiologist before the surgery could be performed.

Before we left the hospital, Father called his primary care physician, Dr. Sini Naik. He told Dr. Naik what happened and that he needed an appointment with his cardiologists at Duke Medical Center. Within three weeks, Father had an appointment.

In the midst of waiting for his surgery to be rescheduled, Father scheduled his prostate antigen examination. On February 10, 2006, Father went to Duke Medical Center for further testing. My father has several health issues—his heart problem being the major issue that included several stents located in his heart due to some of his arteries being clogged. However, other factors might have also contributed to his heart disease. Father led a physically active life, but at age nineteen, he developed high blood pressure. He was obese and had high cholesterol. Nevertheless, the Duke cardiologists monitored his heart condition well. The cardiologists said the spot behind the heart caused no serious complications, so the surgery was rescheduled for the second time.

On Tuesday, February 28, 2006, at 9:00 in the morning, Father was scheduled again for surgery. Again, the family was at his side. We love our parents dearly, and we give one-hundred percent. Our parents cared and provided for us when we were children, and now it's our turn to take responsibilities for them as they become older. That's how God planned this transition for our lives. If we follow God's purpose for us, everything will work out in the end.

Dr. Villani performed a right colectomy. The cancer was contained in the cecum and had not spread throughout the body. The surgery and recovery process went great. Father was hospitalized for seven days. When the final pathology report came back, Dr. Villani recommended chemotherapy as an option for treatment.

My father always asks for my advice in situations of importance. My response was that I couldn't give him any decision about receiving chemotherapy; it had to be his choice. I can only tell him to pray about it and let God guide his steps. God was testing my faith, as I probably would've told Father to take the chemo…or whatever he needed to stay alive. I was being selfish, as I was thinking about me. A question popped into my mind: What would I do without my father?

As a Christian woman, I believe God doesn't like selfish ways or selfish thinking. So I had to pause and take a deep breath before giving Father my response. It's sad when words can affect someone's life and you're thinking only about yourself.

As a child, my father was raised in the church, but he strayed away as an adult. However, he was familiar with God and knew to seek his advice. God is always there in the midst of our troubles to guide and lead us through. Prayer is the answer, and Father must ask God.

friend

I have called you friends, for everything that I learned from my Father I have made known to you...

John 15:15

THE TIME HAS COME

The next Sunday evening, I was reading my Sunday school lesson, and Father called and said he had made a decision. He decided to take the chemotherapy treatments. He was sent to Dr. Mahmood, Oncologist at the Gibson Cancer Center in Lumberton, North Carolina to evaluate his prognosis. Even though the cancer didn't spread to other organs in his body and half of Father's intestines were removed, Dr. Mahmood felt that giving chemotherapy orally would reduce other cancer cells from invading Father's body. Dr. Mahmood informed us there was a ninety-nine point one per cent chance of the cancer returning and the recovery rate was high. He stated that chemotherapy was a preventive measure for some patients.

Two days before Father's sixty-eighth birthday, he began his treatment at the Gibson Cancer Center at 9:45 a.m. on Friday, May 5, 2006. The length of treatment was six months with two weeks on and one week off of the drug. Father was given Xeloda oral medication for the treatment of his colon cancer.

I researched the drug and was aware of all of its side effects. Xeloda is an anti-cancer chemotherapy drug. It is used for metastatic colon, rectal, and breast cancer. It is a pill given by mouth and the amount received depends on many factors, including height and weight, general health or other health problems, and the type of cancer or condition being treated.

There were some things I wanted to know about Father's cancer and Dr. Mahmood was very helpful. He gave Father the highest dose of Xeloda; I questioned his decision. He explained that he gives his patients a high dose to see how well they tolerate the drug, and then, if side effects occur that are intolerable, he would reduce the doses. My father started taking a total of seven pills a day.

Dr. Mahmood explained the stages of colon cancer. He mentioned that there are four stages and Father was in stage two. He said a biopsy will be performed, which is a removal of a lymph node. In Father's situation, four lymph nodes were found and determined to be non-cancerous. Therefore, chemotherapy was recommended to make sure no cancer cells were hidden inside the other lymph nodes.

I was interested in finding out the curable rate for this type of cancer and what blood tests would be performed during Father's visit. The doctor said with stage two cancers, the percentage is 2% - 3%. The cancer spreading to other organs of the body has a percentage of 1% - 3% and a ratio of 1:5 is curable for this type of cancer. My father's blood tests consisted of a complete blood count to check white blood cells, red blood cells, hemoglobin, and platelets. A chemistry panel, which includes a comprehensive metabolic panel and liver function profile would also be performed. In addition, every three months, a carcinoembryonic antigen (CEA) would be performed, which checks the prognosis of the cancer.

For several weeks, Father did fine and he didn't worry about his hair falling out—he didn't have any anyway. My father is a dark, black man, big in size with a large muscular stature. He was handsome with a round face, dark eyes with a visual stare, pearly white teeth and a glowing smile. He loved to cook, and his size indicted he loved food. However, during his treatment, there were certain types of foods he couldn't eat due to changes in his taste buds. His appearance changed, and most of all, his weight was gradually reduced to a smaller size—not skinny but an average size for a big man who once weighed in at two-hundred and eighty-five pounds with a height of six feet, two inches.

On week three, Father's complexion was darker, and with every step his feet were heavier. These types of side effects are known as the "hand and foot syndrome." Its clinical name is Palmar-Plantar Erythrodysesthesia (PPE). The severity range was grades one-to-three for most patients receiving Xeloda. My father's grade was one that was characterized by some numbness and swelling. It didn't disrupt his normal activity so, he continued to work.

When Father was in pain, I felt so sad that I couldn't help him. I came to realize that when a person you love has cancer, you can't begin to understand the emotional trauma they're going through. They are in pain. They are sick. They are sad. In their mind, they understand that the possibility of dying is a part of the illness. What hurts most of all, is that their independence is gone. They have to depend on family members, friends or neighbors. One thing I'm sure of is that life can change in a blink of an eye, but if you stay steadfast in the Lord, He will see you through your darkest days. My father had his Christian family and beloved friends supporting him along the way. He knew somehow, someway that he was going to pull through this storm. God was his rock in times of sickness and sorrow.

I believe God placed stumbling blocks in my life to refocus my mind on Him. If I didn't have trials of illness and affliction, I wouldn't have the need to pray. I learned to trust God and lean on Him when burdened with sadness. He's always there, and as long as I believe in His holy word, my troubles don't seem to be as large as I believe them to be. He will walk with me through my darkest hours. However, one of the greatest comforts to me is to know that someone else has gone through a similar or the same illness as my father and has literally felt the sadness I feel and can help me through my pain. So while my father continues to go through his pain, I trust God as a healer.

With two treatments of chemotherapy for his colon cancer under his belt, Father scheduled an appointment with Dr. Robert Appel, Urologist in Fayetteville, North Carolina, about his prostate antigen examination. It's been four years since his last visit. On his initial visit in March, Dr. Appel told Father that his prostate gland was enlarged. His blood work was drawn and sent to a reference lab to test his prostate level. The doctor's office made an appointment for Father to come back the next week to review the results. Dr. Appel informed Father that his prostate antigen level was elevated. His level was a 4.0 ng/ml. Within two weeks, Father had a biopsy performed on his prostate.

Meanwhile, he was still taking chemotherapy treatments for his colon cancer every other week. On Monday, May 29, 2006, during Father's examination, his lab work was great and his blood pressure 146/85. However, he lost three pounds and was having severe pain in his feet and hands. Dr. Mahmood discontinued his treatment for two weeks and started his chemo again on June 11th by decreasing his doses to 3000 mg/dl. Father always started his chemo drugs on a Sunday morning.

His next appointment was scheduled for June 27th, during which time he was off chemo for two weeks and back on July 9th with the same dose. He skipped one week of medication and started back on July 23rd. Father gained eight pounds, and Dr. Mahmood suggested that he eat Healthy Choice meals. The pain in his feet and hands gradually became severe, and his treatment was changed to every other week—one week of medication and off one week. Father remained on the same regimen of treatment for two weeks since he had no known side effects.

He lost twelve pounds, and his lab results were within normal range. His next scheduled appointment for his colon cancer treatment was August 15, 2006.

THE OUTCOME

On July 24, 2006, Dr. Robert Appel, Urologist, informed Father that his biopsy was positive for prostate cancer. I was angry and wanted to scream, but Father remained calm throughout the whole ordeal. I told Dr. Appel that my father had colon cancer and this couldn't be true. Without hesitation, Dr. Appel told Father that he needed to discuss the options and stages of the disease with him as soon as possible. I asked Dr. Appel how was it possible for a person to have two major cancers in the same year.

He looked dismayed but with a glimmer of hope on his face. By then, I was so hurt and asked God *why my father*. I asked God over and over what was it He was trying to tell me. In the meantime, Father continued to take chemotherapy every other week. He had three more treatments remaining. He wanted to have his prostate surgery as soon as possible. He asked Dr. Mahmood, his oncologist, how long it would take for the chemo to leave his body. Dr. Mahmood told him it would take two weeks. By then, Father had taken five treatments, and the doctor cancelled the sixth one.

It was a hot, rainy day on Friday, July 28, 2006. My mother, my siblings, and I went to Dr. Appel's office with Father. He had a consultation appointment to discuss his options. Meanwhile, Dr. Mahmood decided to discontinue the chemotherapy for Father's colon cancer on August 15, 2006, due to the outcome of his prostate cancer. We arrived a little early for Father's 5:00 p.m. consultation appointment.

We waited until Dr. Appel completed his last patient for the day. Dr. Appel entered his office.

"Good afternoon," he said. He introduced himself to the family, while shaking our hands. He had a serious expression on his face.

During the initial consultation, Dr. Appel explained to Father that the cancer was a 3+3=6 Gleason score. I was aware of what he meant; I'm a medical technologist by profession and I had spoken to one of the pathologists at work about my father's illness. The pattern 3+3=6 Gleason score means that the tumor has only one pattern: the number of the pattern is simply doubled to obtain the score. The cancer was contained in the prostate capsule and no perineural invasion detected. The tumor was a stage T1 grade, which was found in a needle biopsy due to an elevated serum prostatic specific antigen (PSA) level. My father's prostatic level had increased to 11 ng/ml. Sadly to say, the tumor inside Father was growing rapidly.

Dr. Appel explained the severity of the cancer to the family and treatment options. The options were surgery, hormonal therapy, or radiation therapy. Father selected surgery, as it offered the best chance of removing the tumor from the prostate. If the cancer came back after radiation treatments, surgery couldn't be performed due to scar tissue and other adverse effects on the prostate. Hormonal treatments weren't considered, as the family felt that there was less information available and the recovery rate was not as successful in some cases. The best choice was surgery, and the family was in agreement. Dr. Appel told Father that with surgery his sex life would end.

I said out loud, "My father is sixty-eight years old, and if he hasn't had enough sex by now, then it's too late." I wanted Father to enjoy life a little longer with us, and I felt God wasn't ready for him yet. I told Dr. Appel to remove the prostate gland.

My mother, Catherine, looked at me with a smile and started laughing. Then, there was a moment when Father, Mother, and Dr. Appel started laughing together. Nevertheless, I was serious about Father's surgery. I realized that sex isn't everything in life. Growing closer to God is the best love a person can have and without a doubt, my parents were going to continue to love each other with God in their lives.

On Friday, August 4, 2006, my brother, Alvin, drove Father to Carolina Imaging Center in Fayetteville, North Carolina, to get a bone scan. They were running a little late, and I waited outside of the building for them to arrive.

Father's urologist wanted to make sure that the cancer didn't spread to the bone. While Father was undergoing the bone scan, the X-ray technician asked him, "Do you know you have a bullet inside you?"

"Yes," my father said.

My father was shot by his cousin a long time ago, and the doctor couldn't find the bullet. However, twenty-five years later, the bullet was found inside Father without any damage to his organs. This is the power of God that protects us. I wouldn't have known where my strength lies, if I didn't have a relationship with God. To have such an intimate relationship with Him is truly life's greatest blessing. My father had so many decisions to make during his illness. Without God in his life then all of his decisions would have been in vain.

On Monday, August 14, 2006, the bone scan results were found to be abnormal. The radiologist requested a Magnetic Resonance Imaging (MRI) for further studies. The MRI was scheduled for Friday, August 18, 2006. On Thursday, August 24, 2006, Dr. Appel informed Father that the results of the MRI revealed a disc disease. However, cancer wasn't found in his bones. On Friday, August 25, 2006, Father was scheduled to have his pre-test lab done for his prostate surgery at the Diagnostic Center at Cape Fear Valley Medical Center. A week passed, and Father's prostate surgery was getting closer.

Dr. Robert Appel is known as one of the best Urologist in Fayetteville, North Carolina. He exhibits a personality trait that shows a true caring for his patients. He always has a smile and a friendly disposition. You couldn't ask for a better surgeon or doctor to treat your illness.

However, the family knew Father was in the hands of God's care and God would use Dr. Appel's eyes, ears, hands, and other tools provided for Father to successfully undergo surgery.

My mind started to play tricks on me, as the surgery neared. The circumstances or problems that we would face ahead were in God's hands. I clung to the truth of His love for us. In time, my eyes would see the proof of His faithfulness. In the midst of life's fast pace and trials, we easily lose sight of God's love and protection. When we're overwhelmed by trouble, sorrow, or suffering, it's hard to recognize our trust in God.

THE SURGERY IS NEAR

On Wednesday, August 30, 2006, at 7:30 a.m. at Cape Fear Valley Medical Center, Father's operation for the removal of his prostate gland was performed. My mother, Catherine, my brother, Alvin, my sister, Sheila, and I were in the family waiting room. We assumed everything was going all right until we were informed around 9:30 a.m. that Father's condition had worsened. Father's blood pressure dropped, and once his abdominal wall was opened bleeding came from veins that drained his prostate. Dr. Appel believed that there were a lot of adhesions from Father's previous colon cancer surgery that had impacted and complicated his surgery.

Father received several units of blood to stop the bleeding. The family was kept informed about Father's progress. When you realize, and think things are going in your favor, God tests you and knows your thoughts. Dr. Appel had performed many prostate surgeries in his career, but there's always a first with serious complications. Our faith and belief in God would guide Dr. Appel through the operation.

It was approaching noon with no information about Father. We were getting hungry and went to the hospital café to grab a bite to eat. While eating, my cell phone rang. It was my husband, Steve. He called to see how Father's surgery was coming along. I told him that Father was in critical condition. Steve and I continued to talk, vowing to call each other later on in the day. Meanwhile, Mother received a phone call from my nephew, Jevonne.

Mother told him Father was critical. During a quiet moment, while finishing lunch, my sister Sheila's cell phone rang. It was her son, Darrius, who also wanted to know Father's condition. I began to think, *what would we do without cell phones in this hectic life?* Cell phones are so convenient, and without them our busy schedules would never settle down. We used to wait by the telephone to receive calls, and now we have cell phones available twenty-four seven.

Needless to say, God is available all the time. God is there when we least expect His presence. When we returned from the café, I glanced at the clock in the hospital waiting room; the time was 3:00 p.m. Dr. Appel came around the corner and approached us.

"Mr. Gaddy is still very critical and his blood pressure continues to drop."

It was apparent by the expression on Dr. Appel's face that he was somewhat puzzled by what was transpiring in the operating room. While sitting and wondering what to do next, a hospital volunteer called out. "Is the Gaddy family here?"

"Yes," I said.

The volunteer stepped forward. "You have a phone call at the desk."

I left to receive the call. The call was from Uncle Nedward and Uncle Michael, my father's brothers. I gave them an update report about Father. I told them I would keep them informed if anything changed.

Everyone in Fairmont, North Carolina – who knows my father as "Tootie" – called to check on him. Father's supervisor, William, was worried and called twice to see how he was doing. William came to the hospital after he left work and stayed with the family awhile. I realized at that moment, Father was special and that so many people cared about him.

WHAT CAN I DO FOR HIM?

I left the waiting room for a few minutes to get some air. The waiting area was filled with so many people and I felt I needed my quiet space. When I returned to the area where my family was sitting, I looked at them. "It's time to pray," I said.

We got up to go to the hospital chapel. Before doing so, we left a message with the volunteer who was sitting at the desk. We informed her that if anyone should come out of the operating room asking for the Gaddy family, to please tell them we went to the hospital chapel and would be right back. We hurried to the chapel so that we could return back to the waiting room as soon as possible. When we entered, we said our own individual prayer. We knew God was our source of strength. Psalms 119, verse 28 says, "*My soul melts from heaviness; strengthen me according to your word. "* Whatever we prayed for at that moment, we believed God would heal in His own time. His love gave us the words to pray when we were at a loss for our father's illness. We can't find strength in His words if we don't know the scriptures. He opened doors that allowed us to fully receive His comfort.

As we were leaving the hospital chapel, it seemed like a light was shining on our faces. We knew God had answered our prayers. When we returned to the waiting room, the volunteer informed our family that Dr. Appel was looking for us. Just as we started to sit down, Dr. Appel came out of the operating room. It was approximately 5:00 p.m. He said that he had some good news; we smiled. In our hearts, we rested in the knowledge that God had delivered on His Word. Dr. Appel said that Father was in stable condition and that he would be transferred to the Intensive Care Unit (ICU). We asked if we could see him before he was transferred and were allowed to do so for a short while. All of us went back to the recovery room to see Father. He was weak. He struggled to speak, but words would not come out. He smiled. His nurse, Mrs. Susan, informed us that Father lost a significant amount of blood and would be weak and needed to rest. His blood pressure steadily increased due to our presence; so we left and returned to the waiting room.

Nurse Susan stayed with Father until he was admitted to ICU. Her shift was over at seven in the evening, but she refused to leave until Father was transferred to the Unit. She was a special nurse and compassionate about her patients.

It took Father six hours to be transferred. It was around one in the morning before he was situated in the Unit, with Nurse Susan at his side. She didn't reside in Fayetteville; she lived approximately two hours away. She was a dedicated nurse and was determined to stay with us. She escorted the family to the ICU waiting room around one-thirty in the morning.

While in the waiting area, the family decided to leave so we could get some rest for the days ahead. My family lived in Fairmont, which is approximately forty-five miles away from Fayetteville. We were so exhausted from being at the hospital all day. I asked the charge nurse to call me if any changes should occur during the night since I lived nearby. It was difficult leaving Father, but to know God's mercy is to trust His will. Proverbs 3:5-6 in the King James Version reads, *"Trust in the Lord with all thine heart and lean not unto thine own understanding. In all thy ways acknowledge Him and He shall direct thy path."*

I was scheduled to be off from work the following morning. I stopped by the chemistry lab to tell my co-workers about my father's surgery. I met Sharon at the entrance, who told me that Dr. Appel came by the lab looking for me. Sharon mentioned that Dr. Appel was compassionate and greatly concerned about my father's condition. At that moment, Sharon and I started to reminisce about good and bad physicians. I realized that many physicians walk into our lives and show no feelings at all. But when a physician believes the patient came through their illness, not only because of them, the grace of God's miracles are true. Father's physician, Dr. Appel, believed that God was in the midst of everything. Through the hours ahead, I believed Father was going to see better days.

I was finally able to speak with Dr. Appel. He said that Father would remain in ICU until he was stable enough to be transferred to another floor. His body was weak and his blood pressure erratic. Father stayed in ICU for a week. During his stay, he had many visitors and phone calls, to include excellent nurses and professionals that cared. I remember on one visit, Father glanced at me with his sad eyes and said he was tired and wanted to give up.

"Give up? Where is your faith?" I said. "It's a miracle to be alive and God isn't finished with you yet." Father smiled, and my heart filled with joy.

The phone rang; it was my sister inquiring about Father's condition. I told her what Father said, and she started to cry. My sister is a Christian woman, and for her to believe Father was giving up was not acceptable. Immediately, she hung up the phone.

Within a few seconds, my cell phone rang again; it was my nephew, Darrius. He asked what I said to his mother. I told him the same thing I told her—that Father was giving up the will to live. In a quiet silence,

Darrius' voice became weak, and he hung up his cell phone.

Meanwhile, I stayed with Father. My father is a good man, husband, and grandfather. To have all those traits in one person is God's blessing. Days and nights went by but, through it all, God was there. When it seems that nothing can go wrong, something always does. My faith remained strong.

ESCAPE FROM DEATH

In the middle of the week, Father had another scare, and we almost lost him again. He became septic, and a staphylococcal infection invaded his body. He had a high fever, and Dr. Appel was concerned that his kidneys were at risk and could result in renal failure.

Staphylococcus is a group of bacteria that can cause several diseases. It is familiarly known as *Staph* (pronounced staff). Anyone can develop this infection, but Father was at a greater risk. He was a cancer patient and his immune system was weakened due to chemo and surgery. My father said with tears flowing from his eyes, "Daughter, I do not have the strength to continue." He said his body was too tired to fight this battle and he was extremely exhausted. I told Father that I have faith that God will not leave him and only God would keep him here until the end. He smiled through his tears, as I held his hand. I said, "Don't worry, Daddy." At that moment, I started to pray and ask God to please show him the way. My mother-in-law once said, that if we didn't have trials and tribulations in our life, we wouldn't have any reason to pray. Needless to say, my father was so afraid of his sickness that fears weakened his faith. We all have fears. Fears caused me not to believe in God. But God's mercy and grace sustained me and gave me the strength and understanding to continue on. I believe through the storms, God will be there. Trust God, have faith, and see His works.

The next day was a good day for Father. He had several visitors while still in the Unit. My friends, Naomi and Gloria, came to visit for a while. Also, my little adopted sister, Tammy, called and my friend, Tomeshia, from Germany. My father was so happy and grateful to have visitors, as he was so ready to leave the Unit. They asked him how he was doing, and he'd say, "Fine." They talked with me for a few minutes and then left. It's nice to have special friends in your life when you need them the most.

My father received many phone calls and cards from everyone. He wasn't a man of fame and celebrity stature, but in the eyes of all who knew him, he was an icon. The doctors and nurses cared and were compassionate about Father's illness. When a patient is battling two forms of cancer in the same year, it can be emotionally and physically challenging for everyone. Finally, the day came when Father was to leave ICU. He was transferred to 6-South floor—the Oncology unit. While on 6-South, he had many excellent nurses. His sickness became complicated. Dr. Appel was upset and kept apologizing to the family that Father should be feeling better. But I realized that it wasn't any fault of Dr. Appel; he was an awesome doctor. He had Father examined by a cardiologist and gastroenterologist. Father's heart was beating irregular and his stomach was full of gastric content. Every day, a nurse drained the tube from his stomach and cultures were collected when needed. Several lab tests were performed along with EKG's, X-rays, and numerous other blood profiles to evaluate his condition.

One particular day, a lady knocked on Father's door and came in and told him he was going to be all right—she saw angels surrounding his door.

"Oh my God," the woman began, "the Lord's wonderful works is in the midst, and I stopped by to say everything is going to be fine."

From that day, Father showed improvement. He was bedridden and couldn't do for himself. I took on the task of bathing him daily. I could tell he didn't want me to bathe him, but sometimes pride has to take a back seat. Pride can prevent the miracles of God and block communication with Him. I didn't want that to happen to Father.

Father's hospital stay was longer each day. Dr. Appel kept saying he would be leaving soon, but that didn't happen. My father was a complicated case to the doctors, and they were getting frustrated. Dr. Appel and I came to the conclusion that the reason Father was having several problems was the fact that he hadn't been off of his chemo drugs for colon cancer long enough before undergoing prostate surgery. All of his symptoms were reacting with the chemo drugs that remained in his system. Father should've waited a little longer to have the prostate surgery or until the drugs were fully cleared from his body. However, through it all, God brought him through his sickness and made a way.

Father had a scheduled appointment for Tuesday, September 12, 2006, with Dr. Mahmood, Oncologist, in Lumberton. In the meantime, he was still hospitalized at Cape Fear Valley Health System. Dr. Mahmood informed Father that all of his previous scheduled chemo treatments would be cancelled due to the severe complications from the prostate surgery. Father was going through so much stress with his body, and to suggest chemotherapy again was out of the question. Father's next follow-up appointment with Dr. Mahmood was scheduled for December 5, 2006.

During the difficult days ahead, I realized that life holds seasons of despair and seasons of believing that

God is bigger than our problems. In spite of my father's tears, I still heard God's voice saying, peace is with you. While troubling moments surrounded the family, I felt discouraged. There was nothing I could do to take away their pain. Needless to say, my trust in God keeps me assured that every day through our storms His faithfulness is my strength. And on His strength, I will rise above the difficulty. So when life seems to be falling apart and Father's illness is weighing heavily on me, I will continue to lift my head up high to Him where my reassurance comes from.

HOME AT LAST

On Monday, September 25, 2006, Father was discharged from the hospital. He came to the hospital weighing two hundred sixty-five pounds, and during his stay, he gained thirty-five pounds. The tremendous increase in weight was due to fluid intake. However, upon leaving the hospital he weighed two hundred thirty-one pounds with a hospital stay of twenty-six days. His hemoglobin level on discharge was 8.3g/dl; and his body was still weak.

Father was grateful for the many people who came into his life during his stay. He met special people that provided him the best possible care a patient so deserved. The doctors, nurses, technical professionals, environmental services, dieticians, and many others who provided the extraordinary care for Father had shown so much commitment and dedication. However, it was time to start the recovery process at home. I came home for a week to assist Mother with Father's care. Father left with a drainage bag attached to his stomach. It had to be emptied every day, and I was responsible for that task. A home health nurse was assigned to father while the drainage bag was connected to him. She came every day to assure the drainage bag wasn't contaminated and to change the connected plug weekly.

The first week at home, Father's health wasn't better. He was so weak, and his heart was beating too fast. He was taking iron supplements to increase his hemoglobin level; however, he became weaker and weaker. Without hesitation, Mother and I decided to call his primary care physician's office. Dr. Naik was out of town. The nurse told us to bring Father to the office. When we arrived, Father's heart was beating rapidly. An electrocardiogram (EKG) was performed and found Father's heart rhythm irregular. Immediately, the nurse called the rescue squad.

While at the doctor's office, I called one of my Christian friends, Sussie. When I heard her voice, I told her about Father's condition; I started to cry. Sussie said she'd pray a special prayer for my father. At that moment, I felt special to have known a friend who cared. Immediately, I hung up the cell phone and called the entire family. Within an hour, everyone was at the emergency room. Father was admitted to Southeastern Medical Center in Lumberton on October 12, 2006 and was transferred to ICU. The emergency room doctor informed the family that Father's heart was beating too fast and needed to have a cardio version procedure.

The next morning, the cardiologists from Duke Medical Center performed the procedure. They explained that with this procedure, a small electrical shock is delivered to the heart through the chest to stop certain fast arrhythmias, such as atrial fibrillation or tachycardia. These electrical shocks are carefully timed to stop an arrhythmia and restore a normal heartbeat. The procedure was a success, and Father's heart was like new again. If this procedure didn't work, a pacemaker would've been placed into Father's heart. But God's work was in the midst of this circumstance.

God was always with us. He's been the family's deliverance through our darkest days and nights. He's opened our eyes to see His wondrous works. And through our faith, He has shown that He is the greatest. Oh, what a marvelous God we serve. If we take time out of our busy schedules and fit God into the equation, all things will work out for those who serve Him. In the midst of trouble, God was there to provide all we needed and more. He was there when Father needed Him the most because he was giving up. But God spoke to Father and said He wasn't through with him yet.

While hospitalized at Southeastern Medical Center, Father came in contact again with many wonderful people. He was transferred to the Step-Down Unit after having been in ICU for several days. He had a lot of family members and friends, who came to visit; however, he was ready to return home again. His length of stay at the hospital was eleven days, but it seemed like an eternity to him. I stayed with Father and Mother for another week to make sure Father was stable and his condition didn't worsen.

Week one at home was good for father. He regained some strength in his body. His appetite and weight gradually returned to normal. He had a little urinary output and drainage problem. He had to wear men's Depends for a long time, as every time he squeezed, strained, or coughed the lining in his bladder weakened and excessive urine was discharged. However, he continued to show much improvement throughout the following months.

One must come to the realization that life never remains the same, but God's goodness and mercy endures forever. Father was transported to the emergency room on December 4, 2006 at Southeastern Medical Center. He couldn't void any urine and Mother and I were scared. While at the hospital, the ER nurse immediately placed a catheter on Father's right leg until his Urologist in Fayetteville could see him.

He was discharged from the ER and had an appointment to see Dr. Appel on December 12, 2006. The next day, December 5, 2006, Father had an appointment with his Oncologist, Dr. Mahmood. "Your father gained too much weight."

Father's blood pressure and pulse were good. His blood profiles were within normal ranges. Dr. Mahmood requested that Father follow up with his Gastroenterologist to have a colonoscopy screening in April 2007. He said that Father would be on a two-month schedule with him for the next five years. Father's next appointment with Dr. Mahmood was scheduled for February 6, 2007.

RENEWAL OF HIS FAITH

W hen Father was diagnosed with both of his cancers, he didn't complain or even say, *"Why me?"* He accepted his illness and was determined to be a survivor. In order to be healed, Father placed his faith in God, who was the source of hope and strength. As Father grew stronger spiritually and emotionally, the worry that had marked his illness began to vanish. At times, God places us in impossible situations so that we may discover that He is faithful. Father had been in that impossible situation and God gave him a second chance.

Every month, it seemed like Father was going to the doctor's office or to the hospital. But he never got depressed and didn't want to give up anymore. He kept going. With God lifting him up, fighting his battle, and carrying his burden, Father made it through another week. My brother drove Father to Fayetteville for his appointment on December 12, 2006, to see Dr. Appel. I met both of them at the doctor's office. Dr. Appel removed the Foley catheter from Father that was attached to him from his emergency visit a week prior. Father was able to void without difficulty. His urinalysis from the catheter was positive for nitrites and was given antibiotics. A urine culture was pending.

Dr. Appel had a smile on his face. "Your father's prostate level was below the lowest limit and no biochemical evidence of persistent prostate cancer was found." That was great news! During the weeks that followed, Father continued to have episodes of retention problems.

Mother called Dr. Appel's office and was given an appointment for Father for December 29, 2006. Dr. Appel performed a cystoscopy examination on Father in his office.

"Your father had a flap of tissue at the bladder neck," Dr. Appel said, "that may have been acting as a trap door." Dr. Appel performed dilation with filiforms and followers that revealed a wide open bladder neck. The bladder itself appeared to be normal during his observation. Dr. Appel was very hopeful that this procedure would resolve Father's retention problems. Father's next appointment was scheduled for March 20, 2007—a follow-up prostate examination.

Days and months passed until Father's next doctor's appointment. He was doing extremely well. He was even able to return to work. Father was out of work for his colon cancer operation for six weeks and from August 31st through December 15, 2006, for his prostate cancer.

Father returned to work for only a year, as the company was experiencing some cutbacks. He was given an option to retire under the no-work availability status. Father didn't want to leave but realized that life was too short. He wanted to enjoy the rest of his years doing the things that made him happy, and, therefore, he made the decision to retire.

He enjoys sitting in his favorite leather recliner to watch television or riding his bike on sunny days. In the meanwhile, Mother, siblings, and his grandchildren keep him busy, now that his cancer is in remission.

THE STRUGGLE IS OVER

God has been Father's and the family's divine protection during these difficult times. When pain and adversity entered our lives, we knew God wouldn't abandon us. He provided and comforted us in whatever way he saw fit. Every one of us will go through troubling times, and when that happens, it's easy to get disheartened. But remember, God will never leave, and His grace is sufficient to sustain our pain.

The Bible says we should rejoice during difficulty and God will strengthen our faith. We can be joyful in knowing that God is using these circumstances to prepare and grow us spiritually in His word. Nothing that the family and I have gone through these past months, or whatever we may encounter in the future, can take us away from God. He is with us every step of the way. Father retired from work and has been in remission for thirteen years with both of his cancers. Our days of faithfulness carried us through. We still experience God's peace, as He's the only one who can bring peace, joy, and love into our circumstances.

God's Purpose

Some people might wonder why this book was written. Actually, it was a call from God. I don't understand why bad things happen in our lives, but I believe God has a purpose for everything good and bad. He's in control of this world—the beautiful creations and seasonal changes of this earth, as well as my life and yours.

In the midst of our pain, hardships and loss, we cry out, God, why is this happening to us? Sometimes we may receive an answer and sometimes not. But we may rest assured that nothing happens by accident or coincidence. God has a purpose for even our most painful experiences.

Romans 8, verse 28 says, *"And we know that all things work together for good to them that love God, to them who are called according to his purpose." KJV*

He turned my cry into gladness and I've seen His blessings during my darkest hours. So, this was my story to tell about my father's struggle with two major cancers that have taken so many people's lives. There is no secret what God can do—he healed my father. And through faith and prayers, He answered. My fears are gone, and joy came in the break of day.

My family remains faithful in God's mercy and grace and will trust in His goodness. God was our helper and provider in times of our father's sickness; He gave us the strength to continue to pray. My father was walking in the valley of death and wanted to give up. His faith has been renewed, and I recall him saying to me, "*Daughter, I want to live.*"

I simply wanted to share with you my faith that brought me through this crisis. When things get tough, always remember, faith doesn't get you around trouble; it gets you through it. I hope what I've learned along the way will have meaning in someone's life about how God can heal.

The faithful love of the Lord never ends. His mercies never cease. Great is His faithfulness; His mercies begin afresh each morning. (Lamentations 3, verses 22-23 NLT).

Tribute to my father, Ernest P. Gaddy
(as printed in the Fayetteville Observer
June 20, 2010)

The 27th Psalm describes him as the man of circumstances and goodness. My father is my rock of joy, hopes and dreams. God gave him strength to bind our family together. He taught me how to love everybody, regardless if hatred settled within my soul. He is like David; for in the time of trouble, he listens to my every word. He does not judge my outcome because he knows that God is the only man that will judge my life. He raised his children and grandchildren to follow the path of righteousness because when darkness comes, the Lord is our light of salvation. Father always said, "Follow your heart and God will lead you to green pastures. The devil controls your mind and leads you to destruction."

To my father – who has not lived holy his entire life, but remains true to his words – thank you, for your courage, faith, wisdom, kindness and most of all, love for your family.

Happy Father's Day, Daddy.

Your daughter,
Annette Gaddy Harper

ABOUT THE AUTHOR
Annette Gaddy Harper

Annette Gaddy Harper is a graduate of Fayetteville State University, Fayetteville, North Carolina where she earned a B.S. in Medical Technology. She also earned a Master of Science degree in Administration from Central Michigan University in 1990. In 2006, she obtained a Real Estate Broker license from the State of North Carolina Real Estate Commission.

Annette Gaddy Harper was born in Fairmont, North Carolina. Fairmont was once considered one of the major tobacco markets in the world. Annette currently lives in Fayetteville, North Carolina with her husband of over 30 years, Steve C. Harper. She is employed by Cape Fear Valley Health Systems where she has been employed for over 37 years as a Medical Technologist. Her passion is to do for others and to show love to all.

Annette is the author of "Understanding the Clinical Significance of Serum Amylase and Lipase in the Digestive System" which was published in the *Journal of Continuing Education Topics & Issues.* This publication is sponsored by the American Medical Technologists Association.

This is her first book